NELLY THE MONSTER SITTER

THE SQUURMS AT NO. 322

KES GRAY
ILLUSTRATED BY CHRIS JEVONS

HODDER CHILDREN'S BOOKS

First published in Great Britain in 2019 by Hodder and Stoughton
A version of this story was published in Great Britain
in 2005 by Hodder Children's Books

13 5 7 9 10 8 6 4 2

Text copyright © Kes Gray, 2019
Illustrations copyright © Chris Jevons, 2019

The moral rights of the author and illustrator have been asserted.

A CIP catalogue record for this book
is available from the British Library.

ISBN 978 1 444 94441 9

Printed and bound in Great Britain by Clays Ltd, Elcograf S.p.A.

The paper and board used in this book
are made from wood from responsible sources.

MIX
Paper from
responsible sources

TO THE TILLINGHASTS
AT NUMBER TWO

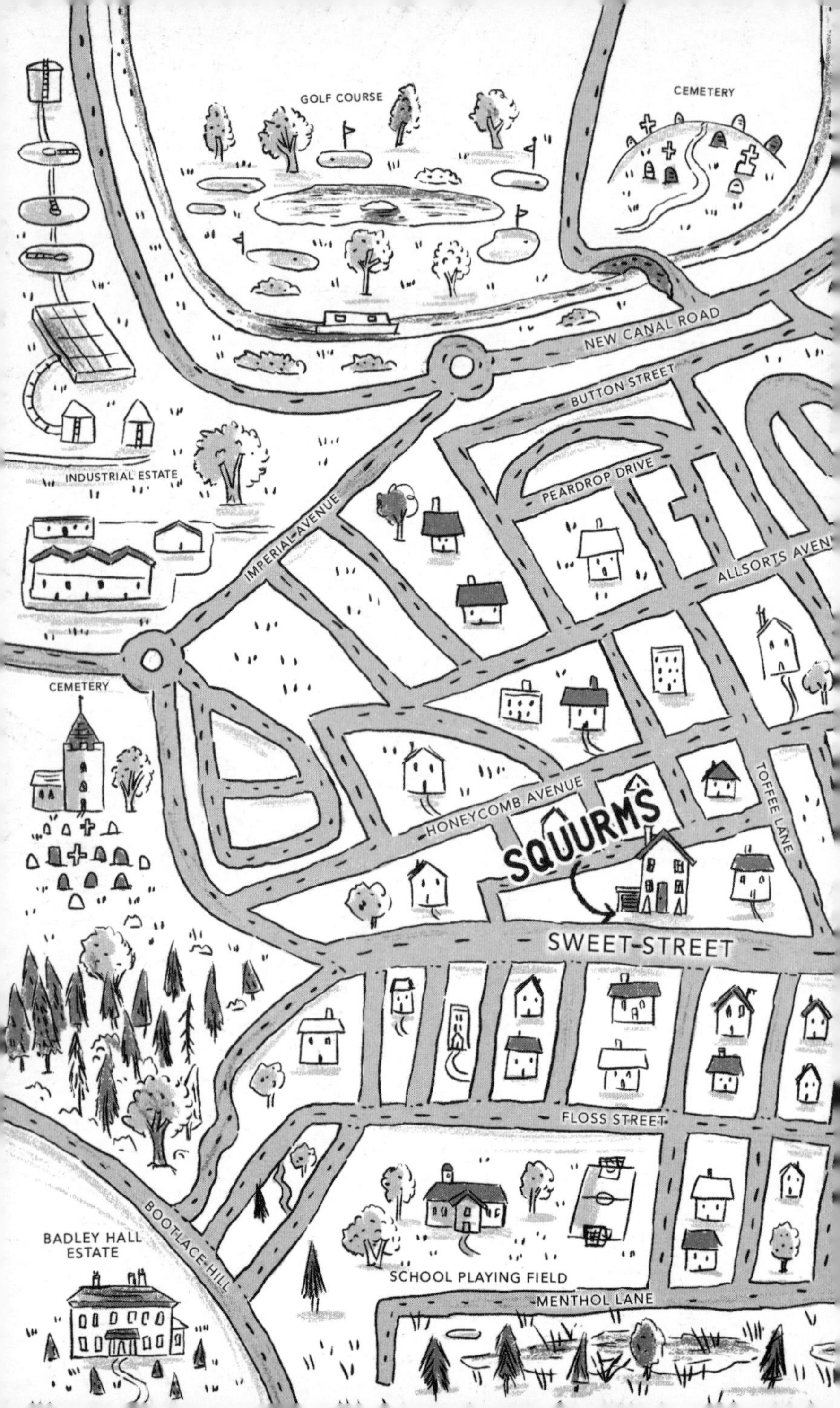
GOLF COURSE
CEMETERY
NEW CANAL ROAD
BUTTON STREET
INDUSTRIAL ESTATE
PEARDROP DRIVE
IMPERIAL AVENUE
ALLSORTS AVENUE
CEMETERY
HONEYCOMB AVENUE
TOFFEE LANE
SQUURMS
SWEET STREET
FLOSS STREET
BOOTLACE HILL
BADLEY HALL ESTATE
SCHOOL PLAYING FIELD
MENTHOL LANE

CHAPTER

Nelly and Asti were arguing again. Not about pop music or TV programmes or the meaning of life. This time it was something far more important. This time it was golden syrup.

'I got it first,' snapped Asti.

'I put it on the table first!' countered Nelly.

The golden syrup lurched backwards and forwards as both sisters wrestled for control of the tin.

'*I'm* not giving in,' grimaced Nelly.

'*I'm* not giving in,' growled Asti.

'If you don't stop arguing I'll tip the rest of this mix down the sink and there won't be any more pancakes for anyone!' threatened Nelly's mum.

Nelly's dad's lip began to wobble. 'But that's not fair. I haven't even touched the golden syrup, I've just had sugar and lemon on mine.'

Nelly's mum paddled her wooden spatula through the pancake mix and sighed.

'Honestly, Clifford, sometimes I wonder who the biggest kid in this family is.'

'They're bigger kids than me,' said Dad, folding his arms indignantly and watching the golden syrup tin ping-pong backwards and forwards in front of his eyes.

'Petronella and Astilbe!' (Mum always called the twins by their christened names when she was cross.) 'If one of you girls doesn't give in both your pancakes will go stone cold and then no amount of golden syrup will make them edible!'

The twins tightened their grips on the golden syrup tin and prepared to battle right through the afternoon and into the night.

'I wish there was no such thing as Pancake Day,' grumbled Mum, ladling another dollop of pancake mix into the frying pan. 'Instead of Pancake Day, there should be 'Twins Go To Bed Early Day' or 'Mums Go Shopping and Spend However Much They Want To Day.'

'Can I volunteer for the next pancake please, love?' asked Dad hopefully. 'I mean, the girls haven't even begun to eat their first one yet.'

Mum flopped the pancake on to her

husband's plate and looked despairingly at her two daughters.

'Smelly Nelly,' lurched Asti.

'Nasty Asti,' lurched Nelly.

'Could you fetch the jam, love, I think I'd quite like jam on this one,' chimed Dad.

Nelly's mum was just about to pour the rest of the pancake mix over her family's heads, pack her bags and start a new life in Hawaii, when the phone rang.

Not the phone in the hallway downstairs but the phone in Nelly's bedroom upstairs.

Although it sounded faint from the kitchen, Nelly's monster sitting phone had a very distinctive trilling ring. And when it rang it only ever meant one thing. Nelly was in demand.

Nelly's eyes detached themselves from the golden syrup tin and craned upwards to the ceiling. How could she answer the phone in her bedroom without giving control of the golden syrup to Asti?

The phone continued to ring.

And ring and ring and ring and ring and ring.

Asti sensed victory. 'Your phone is ringing, Nelly, my sweet,' she cooed, 'and if you don't answer it pretty sharpish one of your scummy hideous ten-headed monster friends won't be able to leave you with one of their freaky monster babies.'

Nelly shoved the tin of golden syrup into Asti's chest and raced out of the kitchen and up the stairs.

'Don't hang up! Don't hang up!' she gasped.

As she burst through her bedroom door she
was greeted by the sound of her own voice.

*'Hi, this is Nelly the Monster Sitter. Please
leave a message after the beeps and I'll get back to
you as soon as I can.'*

Instead of diving for the phone, Nelly let her curiosity get the better of her. She sat down at her homework table with her fingers poised over the phone and waited for the *beep* to *beep*.

The *beep* of the answer phone was followed by a *gurgle* and then a low *gurgling glug*.

Nelly listened intently as the monster on the end of the line began to leave its message.

'Er … hello, Nelly … *gurgle* … Er, we're the Squurms from number 322 … *gloog* … we haven't met before but we've … *glargle* … we've heard a lot of wonderful things about you from Mump and Leech at number 93 … *glurg* … We were wondering if you might be able to monster sit for us this eve—'

Nelly picked up the phone. 'Hello?' she smiled.

Two loud *gurgles* were followed by a *glug* and then a *ning*.

'Is that Nelly the Monster Sitter … *gurgle*?'

'That's me!' said Nelly. 'Of course I'll monster sit for you this evening. What time would you like me to come round?'

The *gurgles* googled and glurgled softly at

the end of the phone and then returned full volume with the answer.

'Could you come at 6.30 and perhaps … *glargle* … stay until 9?'

Nelly glanced at her secret drawer and smiled. 'I'll check with my mum and dad but if you don't hear from me I'll be there right on time. Do I need to bring anything special?'

'Lots of energy!' gurgled the Squurm. 'Our son *gloogle* gets bored rather easily.'

'Is that your son's name, Gloogle?' asked Nelly.

'Pardon *gurgle*,' said the Squurm.

'You said your "son, Gloogle" … is Gloogle your son's name?'

'Our son's name is Slop *gloogle*,' glugged the Squurm.

'Slopgloogle or just Slop?' asked Nelly, who
was beginning to wish she hadn't asked.

'Just Slop *gurgle*,' gargled the Squurm, a
little confused.

'Oh I see, Slopgurgle not Slopgloogle,' said Nelly, trying not to giggle.

'No, just Slop, our son's name is Slop, no gurgles or gloogles, just Slop …' glurgled the Squurm.

'And my name's just Nelly!' laughed Nelly. 'It's very nice to talk to you. I'll see you this evening at 6.30!'

Nelly put the phone down and opened the red fluffy diary on her desk. She removed a strawberry gel pen from her pencil case and carefully added *6.30 Squurms at No. 322* to her monster-sitting diary. She closed the clasp, placed the pen back in its case and swivelled round in her chair. She was just about to lean forward in the direction of her secret drawer when she suddenly sat bolt upright.

'PANCAKES!!' she gasped. Asti was in control of the pancakes!

There was no time to lose. A new entry in her secret monster-sitting notebook would have to wait! The wheels on the bottom of Nelly's office chair spun like a Pookle's eyeballs as she launched herself out of her bedroom and down the stairs.

When she arrived back in the kitchen she found to her dismay that Pancake Day was most definitely over. Her mum was washing up the frying pan, her dad was refilling the sugar bowl and Asti was licking the golden syrup spoon.

'It's all gone,' Asti said with a triumphant lick. 'Gone gone gone,' she said, with three more hugely exaggerated licks.

Nelly's toes curled up inside her shoes. They had a habit of doing that when she was angry. 'You greedy pig!' she snapped at her sister. 'That tin was half full!'

'Now it's two halves empty,' smiled Asti.

Nelly looked at her plate. There was plenty of pattern but a distinct lack of pancake.

'I ate it before it got cold,' smirked Asti. 'Mum said I could.'

'OOHH, MUM!' protested Nelly, placing her hands on her hips and staring daggers at her sister.

'Don't you "Ooh, Mum" me,' said her mum, plunging the mixing bowl into the soap suds. 'What with golden syrup wars and "fetch me the jam", I've had pancakes up to here!'

'Me too,' smiled Asti, pointing to her tummy. 'Actually, I've had pancakes up to here,' she said, moving her hand ten centimetres further up her jumper.

Nelly turned to her dad, but at the mention of jam, he had started limping again. Nelly's dad always limped when he was under attack.

Nelly's toes wouldn't curl any further and so with as much self-control as she could muster she marched out of the kitchen and straight into the hall.

She slapped a Post-it note with the Squurms'
number on to the hallway mirror.

'Where are you off to this time?' called her
dad, responding to the familiar squeaks of
Nelly's marker pen.

'The Squurms at Number 322,' said Nelly,

imagining the mirror was Asti's face and giving the Post-it note one more slap.

'They want me there at 6.30.'

'Have you got any homework to do?' called her mum.

'I haven't, but Asti has!' shouted Nelly, beginning to exact some sweet revenge.

'Don't you "Ooh, Mum" me!' said Nelly's mum, pointing Asti up the stairs in the direction of her room. 'Now go and do your homework.'

As Asti trudged to the bottom of the stairs, Nelly bounced back into her bedroom and closed the door. Her mind was in monster mode now.

'I wonder what Squurms look like? I bet they're hairy. No, they sound slimy. Maybe they're scaly? Where's my purple gel pen? Where's my monster-sitting notebook? Has mum ironed my Sardine sweat shirt?'

'Monster lover!' said Asti, reaching for the handle of Nelly's bedroom door.

Nelly turned the key in the lock.

Click! was her only reply.

CHAPTER

Nelly emerged from her bedroom at 6.15: hair tied back, green jeans, red trainers, Sardine sweatshirt. She glanced towards her sister's bedroom and saw Asti sucking a pencil so hard that her eyebrows had joined in the middle.

'The answer is two,' said Nelly. 'One plus one equals two.'

Asti removed the pencil and stuck out her tongue.

'Two plus two equals four,' smiled Nelly, heading for the stairs.

When she reached the bottom of the stairs she found her dad crouching on his knees and running his hands over the hallway carpet.

'Mind your feet,' said her mum. 'Your dad's lost his contact lenses.'

'They're in the bathroom in their pot,' said Nelly. 'I saw them there ten minutes ago when I was washing my face.'

Nelly's mum turned with a sigh. Nelly's dad stayed low and looked sheepish. 'I could have sworn I had them in,' he said. 'I thought they'd both fallen out when I sneezed.'

Nelly laughed and opened the front door. She felt sorry for her dad sometimes. He always seemed to be one step away from a limp.

'I'll be back just after 9 o'clock,' she said.

'Have fun,' said her mum.

Nelly closed the front door and trotted cheerfully to the end of the garden path. There was a springtime springiness in her step, given extra bounce by the excitement of meeting some new monsters.

She closed the garden gate behind her and turned in the direction of the high even house numbers. No. 322 was going to be some way up Sweet Street to her left, and she would need to cross the road to reach it.

She had decided to stay this side of the road for most of the way and cross further up, but when she saw Natalie Dupre approaching in the distance she decided to cross early. Natalie Dupre was Asti's best friend and as far as Nelly was concerned, that made her someone to be avoided.

Nelly stopped at the kerb and pretended not
to notice Natalie approaching. But wouldn't
you just know it, the very moment she needed

to cross the street, the traffic became so busy in both directions that she became hopelessly rooted to the kerb.

'Hello, Nellsmell!' said Natalie. 'Where are you off to?'

Nelly turned her head with painful reluctance in the direction of Natalie's snake-lipped smile. 'Out,' said Nelly.

'You're not going to babysit one of those freaky deaky monster thingies, are you?' shivered Natalie. 'Asti says they've got twenty heads and huge fangs and no legs and they slime and gunge everywhere and all over the place.

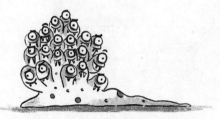

And they eat people or chop you up into pieces with their razor-sharp claws. I hope you've done karate. I wouldn't go anywhere near something like that unless I knew karate.

Asti says sometimes if they're not *that* hungry, instead of eating *all of you* they put giant straws in your ears and just suck your brains out instead.'

'Asti should know,' said Nelly.

'What do you mean?' asked Natalie, her eyes darkening with concern.

Nelly put on her most solemn face. 'The first time I went monster sitting I took Asti with me. The monsters got a bit peckish and Asti got grabbed. I managed to hide under the table, but Asti wasn't so lucky. I actually had to watch as they sucked her brains right out.'

SUCK

SUCK

SUCK

SLURP

'Right down to the very last brain cell.'

Natalie clasped her hands over her mouth in horror. 'Really!' she gasped.

'That's why she can't do maths,' said Nelly, trying to keep a straight face. 'She's got no brain.'

Natalie stood silently beside Nelly and then stared down the road at No. 119. 'What colour was the straw?' she asked.

'Green and white stripy,' said Nelly.

'Asti is in her bedroom right now trying to do her homework – maybe you could help her. Don't say that I told you about the brain removal, will you, because she doesn't want anyone to know.'

Natalie held Nelly's hands in hers and gave them a reassuring squeeze. 'It will be our secret, Nelly,' she whispered. 'I promise I won't say a word or breathe a word. I won't even breathe a single letter of a single word. My lips are totally sealed. Zipped up tight. In fact, I'm only unzipping my lips now because I need to tell you how totally zipped up they are.'

'I must go,' said Nelly. 'Or I'm going to be late.'

'Me too,' said Natalie, hurrying on to offer Asti a lend of her brain.

Nelly waited for a lull in the traffic and then dashed across the road.

She kept the momentum of the run going a full 100 metres further up Sweet Street, only slowing as she approached the houses in the low three hundreds.

312,

314,

316 …

no purple doors yet …

318,

320

…

322.

No purple door at all …

In fact, the front door of No. 322 Sweet Street was plain ordinary white. So plain and so white that if she hadn't had good reason to take a special interest in it, she would have passed it by without even a glance.

Nelly looked around the front garden for clues of monster inhabitants. The privet hedge was neatly clipped, the lawn was nicely kept. There were no two-headed garden gnomes in the borders and no giant milk bottles on the doorstep. When she pushed the front gate open it creaked like an ordinary gate and when she walked down the garden path it felt like an ordinary garden path beneath her feet.

I do hope I haven't got the wrong house, she thought to herself. *I'm sure they said 322.*

She glanced at her watch. It was 6.30 on

the dot. 'Oh well, fingers crossed,' she sighed, smoothing her sweatshirt and reaching up to press the doorbell.

As she pressed the clear plastic button her fingertip sank down into it like a hippo in a swamp. The release of the button was followed by a loud squelch and then topped with the extraordinary sound of a toilet flushing.

Nelly smiled with relief. 'This must be the right house!'

CHAPTER 3

She was still smiling broadly when the front
door flew open, but her eyes widened like
saucers as two monsters oozed into view.

'Hello,' gurgled the Squurm to her right.
'My name's Dollop, and this is my wife, Splat.
You must be Nelly!'

'That's me!' said Nelly, holding out her
hand but then withdrawing it quickly out of
politeness.

As far as she could see, the Squurms had no
hands to shake!

They were like slugs, giant orange upright slugs, with moist glistening bodies and wet foaming mouths. All over their heads, soft yellow eyes nestled like egg yolks. And from their cheeks stiff black whiskers bristled like burnt sparklers.

Nelly smiled politely and waited for the Squurms' next move.

'Give us a squonk, Nelly the Monster Sitter!' gurgled Splat, suddenly sprouting two spaghetti-like feelers and planting them on Nelly's nose.

Nelly's face tingled as two more feelers sprang forward from Dollop's shoulders and fastened themselves to her cheeks. She'd never been kissed Squurm-style before. It was like having your face pressed into a bowl full of cold jelly.

Nelly stepped into the hallway. The doormat was squelchy too. So was the hallway floor. Not sticky squelchy, more bouncy squelchy, like the flooring you get around a climbing frame in a park.

She bounced along the hallway behind the Squurms and then glanced over her shoulder. 'Shall I close the front door?' she said, pointing back.

'I'll get it,' gurgled Dollop, sprouting a four-metre-long feeler and sending it through the air past Nelly's nose.

The front door slammed with a squelch.

Goodness! thought Nelly, following Splat
and Dollop into the lounge. *Exactly how many
feelers does a Squurm have?*

The answer was going up all the time. For there in the middle of the floor, sitting on a white rubber carpet, was Slop. He was only about a metre tall, but what he lacked in height, he more than made up for in circus tricks. Orange, damp and glistening, the cute little Squurm was juggling nine red bananas with six feelers, seven pink apples with five feelers and spinning an aluminium fruit bowl with another.

That's a lot of feelers, thought Nelly, losing count after fourteen. *And that is one clever little monster.*

'Slop, this is Nelly the Monster Sitter!' gurgled Dollop.

'Nelly has come to play with you this evening!' added Splat.

A shower of fruit clattered on to the carpet as Slop withdrew the tentacles back inside his body and began bouncing up and down like a space hopper.

'Ooh glood! Ooh glood!' gurgled Slop, squirming excitedly into a froth of orange bubbles.

'Pleased to meet you, Slop,' smiled Nelly, picking up the fruit and returning it to the fruit bowl.

'Come and sit next to us, Nelly,' gurgled Splat, patting a large green plastic sofa with her feeler.

Nelly lowered her bottom on to the sofa and then toppled over as her bottom slid in three directions at once. 'Is it full of water?' laughed Nelly, trying to settle on the sofa without wobbling too much.

Dollop laughed. 'No, Kipple blubber. It's very comfortable, isn't it, Nelly?'

'Once your bottom eventually stops wobbling!' chuckled Nelly.

Dollop and Splat oozed a little closer and wrapped six affectionate tentacles around her shoulders.

'Now then, Nelly the Monster Sitter, tell us all about yourself.'

'Well,' said Nelly, not sure there was much to tell. 'I live at Number 119 with my mum and dad and my sister.'

'And do they have one head each like you?' asked Dollop politely.

Nelly thought about Asti for a moment and then nodded.

'And how long have you been monster

sitting?' gurgled Splat.

'About six months,' smiled Nelly. 'I love monster sitting, it's brilliant fun.'

'I can see why you would enjoy meeting normal monsters like us,' googled Dollop, 'but don't you find monsters with lots of heads a bit frightening?'

'Two heads are better than one, my mum always says!' smiled Nelly.

'I'm sure you wouldn't say that if you met a Plook,' gurgled Splat. 'All those pink ears and those green and yellow mouths.'

'And those purple eyebrows,' added Dollop with a shudder. 'Plooks give me the wibbles, I can tell you.'

'Never judge a Plook by its cover!' laughed Nelly.

'You're a brave one, Nelly the Monster Sitter. I can see our little Slop will be in safe suckers.'

'Hands,' said Nelly, holding up ten fingers. 'Humans say "safe hands".'

'Squurms say "safe suckers", but tonight it will be safe hands!' gurgled Splat, waving two feelers playfully in front of Dollop's nose.

'How old is Slop?' asked Nelly.

'He's five and a bite,' googled Splat.

'Don't you mean "five and a bit"?' asked Nelly.

'No, his teeth have started to come through now. He's five and a bite. Show Nelly your teeth, Slop.'

Slop tilted six yolky yellow eyes up at Nelly and parted his thin black inner tube-like lips into a smile.

Two rows of lime-green barracuda-style
teeth presented themselves to Nelly.

'He may only be five and a bite,' continued Splat, 'but he's very advanced for his age. He can already count from a trillion to one backwards and he can do his eighty-three times table just like ...' Nelly leaned back as Splat clicked another feeler in front of her nose ... 'that!'

'That's incredible,' said Nelly. 'My sister is still learning her one times table.'

Nelly smiled at Slop and then leant forwards to examine her shoelaces. Slop had tied them together.

'Hah, so you're a practical joker, are you?!' she laughed. 'I'm not falling for that one!'

Slop's eyes glowed orange for a moment and then faded back to yellow.

'The trouble is, Nelly,' gurgled Dollop, 'because he's so bright, Slop gets SO bored SO easily. Do you think you'll be able to keep him amused while we're away?'

'Entertainment is my middle name!' smiled Nelly, retying her laces and then sliding off the sofa with a squelch. 'We'll be fine, won't we, Slop?

'What are we gloing to play, Nelly?' gurgled Slop, his orange body rippling like the blob in a blob lamp.

'There are plenty of games in the cupboard under the window,' gurgled Dollop.

Nelly sat cross-legged on the floor.

'It's far too nice an evening to play indoors!' she laughed. 'I think we should go out into the garden, don't you, Slop? Maybe we can make up some games of our own!'

Slop began to froth with excitement and pointed all six eyes towards the garden.

Splat stood up with a blubbery squish.

'Dollop and I thought we'd go to the cinema, Nelly,' she gurgled, 'We've never been to see a movie in a cinema before! I'm just going upstairs to put on my make-up and then we'll be ready to leave.'

Nelly adjusted her scrunchee. 'We'll be outside if you need us,' she smiled. 'Come on, Slop. Show me where the garden is. It's time to have some fun!'

'Thish way, Nelly!' Slop frothed excitedly, sprouting a long sinuous feeler and attaching it like a limpet to her chin.

Nelly scrambled to her feet and let her chin

lead the way. Across the soft rubbery white tiles of the lounge she skipped, through a glistening curtain of silver beads and into another room at the back of the house.

She could see the garden beckoning through the open French doors, but suddenly applied the brakes. The soles of her trainers squeaked as she skidded to a halt on the rubber carpet.

'Whoah, Slop, whoah!' she laughed. 'What have you got there?'

Slop squelched to an impatient halt and turned round. His yellow yolky eyes travelled the length of Nelly's outstretched arm and came to rest on the tip of her pointing finger.

'It'sh our fish tank,' said Slop, releasing Nelly's chin with a soft *thwuck*.

Nelly peered wide-eyed at the biggest home aquarium she had ever seen. It was at least three metres long and a metre deep, and it was supported by an industrial-strength stand

made of scaffold poles.

'That glass must be ten centimetres thick!' gasped Nelly, tapping the front wall of the aquarium with her finger.

It needed to be. The moment Nelly's finger tapped the glass, a shoal of ferocious yellow creatures flew out from behind a pile of house

bricks, hurled themselves in her direction and
began barking at the glass.

Yes … *barking* at the glass.

Nelly withdrew her finger instantly and watched in astonishment as the barking turned to growls.

She'd never seen or heard fish like them. They were about the length of a fish finger, but the similarity ended there. Some had two heads, some had three tails and there was a distinct lack of breadcrumbs. Across the tops of their backs was a crest of black needles and along both flanks of their bodies were ridges of flapping red fins.

'What kind of fish are those?' Nelly gasped.

'Shreddas,' yawned Slop.

'They look hungry,' said Nelly, leaning forward for a closer inspection and then stepping back as the growls erupted into barks again.

'They're always hungry,' sighed Slop. 'Don't put your fingersh in the tank, whatever you do!'

'What do you feed them on?' asked Nelly, taking another cautious step away from the aquarium glass.

'Piranhas,' yawned Slop. 'Come on, Nelly, fish tanks are boring. Let'sh go into the garden and play.'

Nelly quivered slightly as another cold damp Slop sucker attached itself to her right ear and gently drew her away from the aquarium.

I wonder if they eat Astis as well as piranhas, she thought, glancing back at the Shreddas. *I wonder if you can get them from the pet shop?*

Six sideways steps and a tug later and she was through the French doors and into the garden.

'What shall we play, Nelly?' frothed Slop.

'What shall we play?'

Nelly scanned the garden. There was a big lawn and some trees to climb – plenty of play potential.

'Be careful in the sandpit, Nelly, it's very deep!' gurgled a familiar voice.

Nelly turned to find Splat and Dollop standing by the open French doors.

If they'd looked unusual when she first met them, they looked even more unusual now.

'How do we look, Nelly?' gurgled Splat. 'How do you like our glow-in-the-dark make-up?'

'And glow-in-the-dark toothpaste!' frothed Dollop.

'Well, you're certainly going to stand out in the cinema!' laughed Nelly.

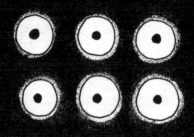

'You'll probably be a bigger attraction than the film!'

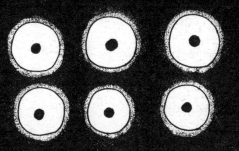

Splat's cheeks blushed blue with embarrassment. A twiddle of feelers rippled in all directions and then pointed in the direction of the lawn. 'Seriously, Nelly, please be very careful if you play in the sandpit. The sand goes all the way down.'

Nelly smiled at the sight of a harmless-looking square of sand a couple of metres from the patio.

'It's OK, I've played in sandpits before!' she laughed.

'It's time we went, dear,' gurgled Dollop. 'Or we'll miss the film.'

'What film are you going to see?' asked Nelly.

'Toxic Scum Revenge Attack 3,' gurgled Splat. 'I do so love a good romance.'

'Don't forget to have an ice cream in the interval,' Nelly grinned.

'We're going to have six!' gurgled Dollop.

Nelly waved with her free hand as the Squurms departed from the garden.

'Goodbye, Nelly!' they gurgled.

'One more thing, Nelly,' they gargled, returning to the garden almost as quickly as they had gone.

'There's one thing we forgot to tell you about playing games with Slop,' gurgled Dollop.

'Oh yes, what's that?' smiled Nelly.

'Slop likes to win,' gurgled Splat.

'Slop has to win!' gurgled Dollop.

'We'll see about that!' laughed Nelly.

CHAPTER 4

With the front door of No. 322 finally closed and Dollop and Splat finally on their way to the cinema, Nelly and Slop were left alone in the garden to play.

'Have you ever played bat and ball, Nelly?' gurgled Slop excitedly.

'Of course I have,' Nelly replied. 'I'm rather good at it, actually.'

'I've never losht to anyone at bat and ball!'

Nelly smiled to herself. She was pretty handy with a bat and ball herself.

'Catch!'

Slop gurgled.

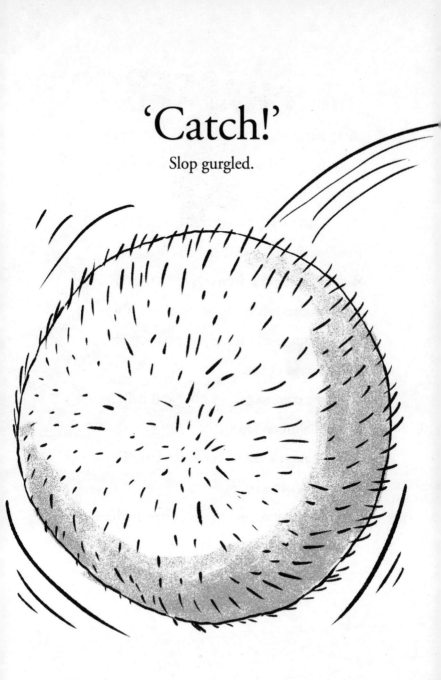

Nelly ducked as a dozen white balls catapulted out of the shed thick and fast, landing like a shower of giant hail stones around their feet.

'I wasn't ready!' said Nelly, a little bamboozled by so many balls firing at her at once and a little embarrassed not to have caught a single one.

'I'm gloing to get the bat,' smiled Slop, sending all twenty feelers back to the shed and then stretching each one to breaking point.

'He doesn't want to play,' frowned Slop, leaning back forty-five degrees and straining with every sinew. 'What a grumpy bat he is!'

Nelly's eyes switched from the shed at
the end of the garden to the balls scattered
around the patio. She was beginning to get the
feeling that this could be bat and ball with a
difference.

'Can you help me pull, Nelly?!' gasped Slop, digging in like a one-man tug of war team in an attempt to dislodge the bat from the shed. 'We can't play bat and ball without a bat.'

Nelly dropped to her knees and then gingerly wrapped her arms around Slop's waist. It was like hugging a slimy marshmallow.

'After three, pull!' strained Slop.

'We can play something else, if you like,' said Nelly, not entirely sure that Slop's idea of bat and ball was a good idea.

'No, no,' said Slop, 'we have to play bat and ball, bat and ball ish one of my favourite games!'

'One, two, three, PULL!'

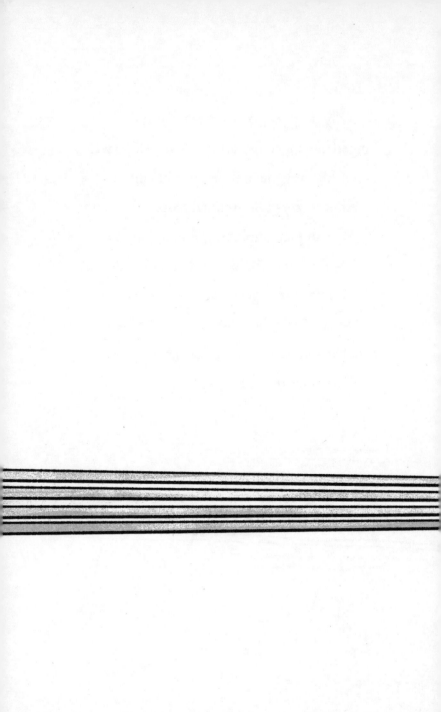

'What was that?' gasped Nelly, as a high-pitched scream issued from the end of the garden.

'That's the bat,' winced Slop, sending some more feelers spiralling up the garden and into the shed. 'Bats don't like playing in the daylight.'

Nelly gave up with the questions and just pulled. Whatever was about to happen was bound to be totally weird – after all, she was a monster sitter and when you monster sit, weird becomes totally normal.

One explosive moment later, she was flat on her back with a jubilant Squurm bouncing up and down on her chest.

'He'sh out!' Slop shouted excitedly. 'The bat is out of the shed!'

Nelly shuffled backwards fast. Slop was right. The bat was most definitely out of the shed.

And it didn't look happy at all.

CHAPTER 5

Ultraviolet eyes, flared dragon-like nostrils, wings the texture of black velvet curtains and a wingspan the size of a microlite … it was the biggest bat Nelly had ever seen.

'These are your balls, Nelly!' said Slop,
jumping up and down like a space hopper and
corralling the white balls into two piles with
his tentacles. 'We've got ten each!'

Nelly turned her head towards the balls
piled up beside her and then brushed some
with her fingertips. They were white as snow,

the size of coconuts but had the short bristly feel of freshly trimmed hedgehogs.

'OK, Nelly, you throw first!' gurgled Slop. 'You throw first and I'll throw second.'

Nelly was completely lost now. She was sitting on her bottom on a lawn with a giant bat in front of her surrounded by prickly balls that she wasn't sure whether to roll, throw, bounce or bowl.

'Hang about,' she said, climbing to her feet in an attempt to take control of the situation. 'It might help if you told me how to play first.'

Slop stopped bouncing with a squelch.

'I thought you knew how to play bat and ball?' he frowned.

'I do know how to play bat and ball!' Nelly insisted. 'Only not this kind of bat and ball!

The kind of bats I play with have handles not wings!' she exclaimed.

'How weird,' shrugged Slop. 'Why would you want a bat to have a handle?'

'To help you hit the ball!' said Nelly. 'Without the handle you wouldn't be able to hit the ball with the bat!'

'But you're not meant to hit the ball with the bat,' said Slop, getting a little agitated. 'You're meant to hit the bat with the ball! Why would anyone want to hit a ball with a bat?' he asked, working himself up into a bit of a lather.

'Because that's the way humans play bat and ball!' said Nelly.

'Well, it'sh not the way monsters play bat and ball,' frothed Slop.

'I KNOW!' gasped Nelly. 'That's why I'm asking you to tell me the rules!'

'Hitting a ball with a bat ish just plain silly,' continued Slop, struggling to get his head around the absurdity of Nelly's version of his favourite game. 'Anyone can hit a ball with a bat. Hitting a bat with a ball ish much harder,' he frothed. 'And more fun,' he lathered, 'and more exciting,' he bubbled.

'Then tell me the rules!' gasped Nelly.

Slop composed himself, wiped the froth and bubbles from his body and then pointed a tentacle down the garden. 'That's a bat,' he explained.

'I know it's a bat,' said Nelly, folding her arms indignantly and waiting to hear something she didn't know.

'And thish is a ball,' said Slop, attaching a
sucker to a ball from his own pile and spinning
it like a basketball in front of her nose.

'I see,' said Nelly, deciding it was better to play dumb. 'And how do you hit the bat with the ball?'

'By throwing it,' said Slop. 'By throwing it at the bat.'

Sounds simple, thought Nelly, sizing up the giant bat and growing increasingly confident in her ability to score a bullseye every time.

'Not just any part of the bat, though,' continued Slop, 'you only score points if your ball hits one of the targets.'

Nelly frowned. Things were starting to get a little more complicated now.

'What targets?' she asked.

'The targets underneath its wings,' said Slop, with a click of his tentacle.

Nelly jumped back and then did a double take.

'You mean, those targets?' she gasped.

'That's right!' said Slop. 'The targets on the bat are hidden before the game starts but you can see them as soon as it flies!'

'The bat flies?' frowned Nelly.

'Of course the bat flies!' said Slop. 'That'sh why it has wings and not handles!'

'Is there anything else it does?' asked Nelly, keen not to sound any more foolish.

'It dodges!' said Slop. 'As soon as you throw your first ball it will fly into the air and dodge out of the way! It's really glood at dodging, Nelly, you'll need to do really fast throws.'

For the first time since agreeing to play bat and ball, Nelly was beginning to understand the game she was about to take part in.

It's like dodgeball, she smiled to herself. She had played dodgeball during PE at school. And she wasn't half bad at it either!

'So all I have to do is hit the targets?'

'That'sh all you have to do!' smiled Slop. 'Five points for the outer ring, ten points for the middle ring and fifty points for a bullseye!'

Nelly bent down and closed her fingers around her first ball.

'How will you know what my score is?' she asked.

'The balls will shtick to the targets,' frothed Slop. 'The targets are prickly like the balls, which means we can count up your score at the end.'

It's like Velcro! thought Nelly, *the balls and the targets on the bat's wings stick together like Velcro!*

'Highest score wings!' she laughed, extremely pleased with her own joke.

'No, Nelly,' frothed Slop missing the joke completely. 'Highest score *wins* not *wings*.'

'Whatever,' Nelly sighed, taking aim with her first ball. 'Let the game commence!'

CHAPTER 6

The instant Nelly arched her eyebrows, the bat began to glare.

'He doesn't look very keen to play,' she whispered.

'That'sh because he knows how glood I am at bat and ball!' frothed Slop. 'You throw your ten balls first, and then I'll show you how it'sh done.'

'No lessons needed, thank you,' murmured Nelly under her breath.

With a deep breath she focused on the

target to her left, turned her body to one side and then hurled the ball hard and fast.

SNAP! went the wings of the bat, removing the targets from view and then launching itself into the air.

'Missed!' laughed Slop, bouncing up and down on the lawn. 'I told you you had to do glood throws!'

It wasn't just a miss. It was a miss by a mile. In spite of its size and in spite of its reluctance to join in the game the bat had the reflexes of … well, a bat.

Nelly gulped, reached for another ball and stared squarely up at the sky.

The bat was suspended directly above her head, wings outstretched, targets beckoning.

Blam! she went, feigning to throw right but then hurling her ball at the left target instead.

The bat took to the sky in a blink,
consigning her ball to the roof of the shed.

'Missed again!' frothed Slop. 'Only eight
balls left, Nelly, then it's my turn!'

Never mind your turn, thought Nelly, *I
haven't got my eye in yet.*

It was time for a change of tactics: two balls,
one in each hand, and some super-rapid fire.

BLAM BLAM!! she went, spinning like a typhoon, feigning left, dodging right, and then hurling two balls in quick succession.

The bat darted left, right, left and then upwards and over, sending both balls whistling into thin air.

'It's using sonar,' gulped Nelly. 'It can feel my balls coming before it even sees my balls coming!'

'Six balls left!' chuckled Slop, sprouting six feelers. 'Would you like me to hand them to you?'

Nelly nodded and lowered her eyes to waist height. Her remaining six balls were now balancing on the end of six obliging tentacles, ready to be grabbed, ready to be launched.

If her eyebrows were arched with determination at the beginning of the game, they were as bent as hairpins now.

She had decided to switch to Jedi mode, to unleash a whirlwind of *blams* that were so blammy, the bat wouldn't have time to *d*, let alone *odge*.

'Thanks, Slop,' she said, closing her fingers around ball number five and passing it to hand number two. 'Keep 'em coming,' she said, re-arming her right hand and then arching her back skywards.

The bat was hovering just two metres from her face, even worse it was stifling a yawn. Its wings were outstretched and its targets on tantalising display. The outer rings were the size of dustbin lids, the inner rings the size of manhole covers, the bullseyes had the circumference of a saucer. With lightning speed, Jedi moves and good old 'trust the force' luck, Nelly was sure she could post a decent score.

'After five, Slop,' she shouted, staring the bat above her squarely in the eyes. 'The moment I count to five, Slop, pass me those balls as though your life depends on it.'

Slop's body began to lather and his tentacles began to straighten.

'Will do, Nelly,' he frothed.

ONE ...

TWO ...

THREE ...

It was a genius move, a cunning, desperate, low-down and dirty tactic, that was so underhand and so surprising, even Nelly barely saw it coming. On the count of THREE, not the count of five, she had suddenly unleashed a five-ball aerial assault that was so rapid and so forceful, her hands almost detached themselves from her wrists.

'Maybe they didn't stick,' panted Nelly, staring up at the empty targets.

'They always shtick,' chuckled Slop. 'You just missed, that's all. Wait till my go and I'll show you!'

Nelly looked around the garden and began counting her wayward balls. There were four on the lawn, two by the fence, three on the shed roof and one on the patio behind her. Slop was right, from a distance of just two metres she had missed with every single throw.

'Watch and learn, Nelly,' bubbled Slop, with a click of his feeler, 'watch and learn!'

CHAPTER 7

At the sound of the *click* the giant bat returned obediently to the lawn and stretched out both its wings.

'Why have its eyes turned red?' asked Nelly.

'I've told you,' said Slop, 'it knows how glood I am at bat and ball!'

Nelly stepped forward for a closer look.

'He doesn't like to be touched,' said Slop.

'I won't touch,' said Nelly, 'I'll just look.'

'Nice batty,' she said, walking forward but deciding to keep a safe distance.

A nice batty it wasn't. The moment Nelly's mouth broke into the friendliest of smiles its teeth bared like a guard dog's.

Nelly took an extra step back for safety and peered as closely as she could at the underside of each wing. Her Velcro hunch was right. Each of the rings on both of the targets looked to have the texture of a scrubbing brush; the rest of the wings were black but picnic-blanket smooth.

'I guess my balls would definitely have stuck if I'd been on target,' she conceded, turning on her heels and rejoining Slop in the throw zone.

'Definitely,' frothed Slop. 'Now watch how it'sh done.'

Nelly folded her arms and stepped back on to the patio for a better view.

'Ready?' frothed Slop.

'Ready,' said Nelly.

'I wasn't asking you, I was asking the bat,' said Slop. 'I like to make sure it has a fair chance.'

The eyes of the giant bat glowed as red as hot coals and its black hairy legs bent low in anticipation of a fast take-off. But take off it most certainly didn't.

BLAM BLAM BLAM BLAM BLAM BLAM BLAM BLAM BLAM BLAM BLAM!!!

And it was all over.

If Nelly had blinked, she would have missed it. Even though she didn't blink, she still missed it. Or rather them. Ten balls, ten feelers, ten micro-blinks of a second and Slop's go had ended.

Nelly stared at the bat, or rather at the targets on the underside of its wings.

Before they had had time even to flap, Slop had completely nailed them with all ten balls.

'One-nil to me, Nelly! Do you want to play again? I've got some more balls in the shed!'

Nelly opened her mouth to speak, but couldn't find the words.

'I'll put the bat away,' gurgled Slop. 'Then we can play something else!'

Nelly stared dumbstruck from the patio as

Slop led the bat back to the shed. Was what she had just seen, or rather not seen, even possible? She'd heard of the speed of sound and the speed of light, but the speed of Slop was something else.

'You haven't got swingball, have you, Slop?' Nelly called as Slop returned from the shed. 'That's the sort of bat and ball game I like best.'

'The children next door have,' he frothed. 'I've watched them playing it from my bedroom window. It'sh a ball on a rope, isn't it?'

Nelly nodded and then laughed as Slop sprouted a dozen feelers and pretended to play swingball in front of her, jumping from left to right and taking imaginary swipes at the air. He looked like a demented cheese string.

'I think swingball would be better if it had a hundred balls on a hundred ropes!' frothed Slop.

Nelly gave up and turned her attention to the sandpit.

'Have you got any buckets and spades?'
she said. 'We can have a sandcastle-building
competition!'

Slop scratched his shins with three feelers. 'I'm not sure it'sh the right sort of sand for sandcastles,' he gurgled.

'Don't worry,' said Nelly. 'If it's too dry, we can add some water from the sink in the kitchen.'

She crouched low and smiled. 'I haven't been in a sandpit for years!' she giggled, throwing her arms above her head and jumping in with both feet, ankles, shins, knees, thighs, arms and shoulders.

'GERONIMO!' she cheered.

'SLOP!' she squealed. 'I'M SINKING!'

Nelly wasn't just sinking, she was sinking fast!

'It's quicksand, Slop! It's quicksand!' she gasped. 'I'm being sucked under, please help!'

Slop jumped into the sandpit and began
to paddle around playfully on his back. For a
Squurm it was nothing more than a paddling
pool.

'What's a sandcastle?' he asked.

'I'm not playing, Slop, I'm not playing! I'm sinking!!'

'Ohh gloodness!' gurgled Slop, sprouting thirty feelers all at once.

Twelve feelers slapped themselves to the top of Nelly's head, three fixed themselves to her cheek and nose, two more to her ears and the rest to a tree over by the fence.

With an incredible heave and a noise like a Bog belch, Slop dragged Nelly from the quicksand and dumped her in a heap back on dry land.

'Thank you, Slop!' she panted. 'That wasn't the sort of sand I was expecting! How deep does it go down?'

'Two kilometres is the furthest I've ever been,' gurgled Slop.

'I think maybe we should play indoors,' panted Nelly.

'I don't mind where we play, Nelly,' gurgled Slop. 'As long as I have a chance to win!'

CHAPTER 8

Nelly padded across the black rubber flooring, past the Shredda tank and back into the lounge.

'I feel like I've been stretched like a rubber band,' she groaned.

'I'm glood at stretching,' said Slop.

'Who taught you to juggle?' said Nelly,
plucking an apple from the fruit bowl.

'I taught myself,' gurgled Slop, cartwheeling on four feelers.

'Can you do this with your tongue?' said
Nelly, rolling her tongue like a newspaper and
wiggling it about.

'I haven't got a tongue,' gurgled Slop. 'Can
you do thish with your eyes?'

Nelly watched as Slop jolted his head
forward sharply, sending all six of his egg-yolk
eyeballs dangling from their sockets. They

bounced up and down in front of Nelly like globules of glue before catapulting back into place with another sharp flick.

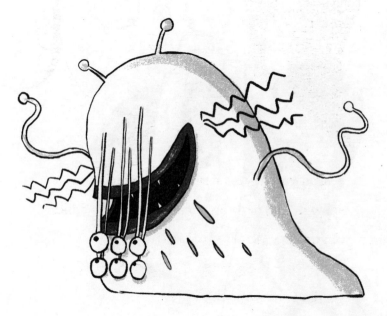

'You're good!' grinned Nelly. 'You're very good. But can you do this?'

Slop watched intently as Nelly placed both hands behind her back, interlocked her fingers and then passed both hands back over her head again.

'I'm double-jointed,' smiled Nelly.

Slop grew eight feelers, twiddled them together like twine, passed them over his head, wrapped them around his waist and then draped them around his neck like a scarf.

'I'm no-jointed,' he grinned.

'You win!' laughed Nelly, somersaulting across the floor towards the games cupboard beneath the window.

It wasn't her best ever somersault, but she was running out of tricks that Slop might not be able to do.

'I always win!' boasted Slop with a somersault of his own.

'I'm Slop, champion games player of the world! Undefeated, unbeatable, unbelievably good at every single game that has ever been invented!'

'We'll see about that!' said Nelly, prising open the two white plastic doors of the games cupboard.

It was full of games. All of them monster-strange.

'How do you play this?' asked Nelly, pulling a purple and red stripy tube out of the cupboard.

'You need eight legs to play that one,' gurgled Slop.

Nelly returned the tube to the cupboard.

'How about this one?' she asked, pulling a silver and green board out of an aluminium box.

'Not suitable for creatures with one brain,'
said Slop. 'These are all monster games, I'm
afraid, Nelly – you have to be normal to play
them.'

Nelly frowned indignantly. 'What are you
saying, Slop? One head, two arms and two legs
sounds perfectly normal to me!'

'Well, not to me, it doesn't!' gurgled Slop.

Nelly frowned into as many of Slop's eyes as she could see at once, held her breath for as long as she could, then burst out laughing.

'Haven't you got any normal games – sorry, I mean weirdo games?' she asked.

Slop scratched the middle of his chest with three feelers and thought hard. 'Do you know what, Nelly! I believe there may be some weirdo games in the cupboard under the stairs. My mum found a whole pile of weird shtuff in the attic when we moved here.'

'Let's take a look!' said Nelly.

She followed Slop out of the lounge and into the hallway. 'They're in here,' gurgled Slop, pointing under the stairs.

'There's no handle on this cupboard either,' frowned Nelly.

'Squurms don't need handles,' gurgled
Slop, planting a sticky feeler pad
against the chromium
panel and wrenching
it open with
a *thwuck*.

Nelly waited patiently as Slop sent eight more feelers into the cupboard.

'Here they are,' gurgled Slop, pulling three large carrier bags out of the darkness.

'Excellent!' said Nelly, dropping to her knees and plunging her hands inside the first bag.

'Well, we can't play kettle and we can't play saucepan,' said Nelly, rummaging through the contents. 'Or flower pot or toasted cheese sandwich maker or bread board. Let's have a look in the second bag.'

Slop hurled the first bag back under the stairs while Nelly reached inside the second.

'TWISTERRRRR!!' she cried. 'You've got Twister! Oh, I love Twister. You'll love Twister!'

'How do you play Twister?' gurgled Slop, a little intrigued.

Nelly opened the box and explained.
'Basically, you spread this mat out on the floor
like this, and you have to stretch your arms and
legs across all these different coloured circles
and get in a right tangle without losing your
balance. If you lose your balance and fall over,
the other person wins!'

'I win again,' gurgled Slop.

Nelly watched dumbfounded as Slop sprouted more feelers than a sea anemone and placed them effortlessly on every coloured circle on the Twister mat without losing his balance in the slightest.

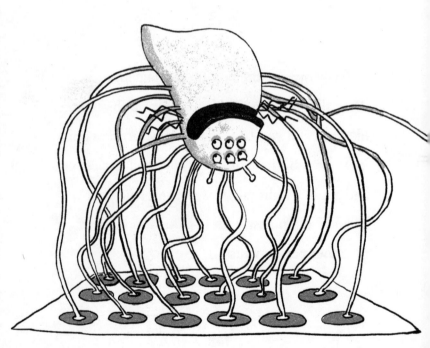

'I can take your goes too if you like!'
laughed Slop, producing one extra feeler to
tickle Nelly under the chin with.

'OK, maybe Twister isn't for us,' she sighed.
'I'll see what else is in the bag.'

There was a china poodle, a loo brush, a thermos flask and a big-value king-size box of soap powder.

Nelly reached for bag number three.

'AHAAAA!!' she whooped. 'You can have all the arms and legs in the world but it won't help you beat me at Scrabble!'

Slop slithered up close as Nelly pulled a Scrabble box out of the bag and laid the board out on the floor. She emptied the letters into one of the carrier bags and gave them a shake.

'Are these the instructions?' gurgled Slop, passing the lid of the box in front of three of his eyes.

'Yup,' said Nelly. 'Would you like me to read them to you?'

'I've just read them,' chuckled Slop, reaching into the bag with a long sinuous feeler and drawing the letter **J**.

Nelly placed her hand in the bag, pulled out her letter and peered at it.

'**E**! ... **E** is lower than **J** so that means I go first!'

'OK,' gurgled Slop, unphased by Nelly's

early advantage.

Nelly took her first seven letters and arranged them on her rack. Slop plunged seven feelers into the bag and took out his letters too.

After much frowning and lip-nibbling, Nelly placed her first word on the board.

'**F A R M** … that's twelve points to me.'

'Is it my go now?' gurgled Slop.

'Yes,' said Nelly, placing four new letters on her rack.

'Thirty-eight points to me,' gurgled Slop, placing all seven of his letters down on the board. 'Plus fifty for a seven-letter word.'

Nelly placed her hands on her hips.

'**JAFUKOOG**? What kind of a word is **JAFUKOOG**?'

'It'sh Squurmese for "thank you",' gurgled Slop, reaching into the bag for another seven letters.

'Oh,' said Nelly, writing down Slop's score and then frowning intensely at her letters.

After three long minutes, her face broke into a smile.

'**JELLY**,' she pronounced triumphantly. 'Seventeen points to me!'

'104 to me,' gurgled Slop, placing seven more letters down on the Scrabble board.

'**GONZIBOX**? What's **GONZIBOX**?' exclaimed Nelly.

GONZIBOX

'It'sh where Squurms keep their fish food,' gurgled Slop, adding his score to the pad.

'I thought you said you fed your fish piranhas?'

'We do,' gurgled Slop, 'but we keep our piranhas in a gonzibox.'

'Oh,' said Nelly, sensing that her heaviest ever Scrabble defeat was approaching.

Slop was as good at Scrabble as he was at

WE

bat and ball. Nelly learnt
that a **QUAILFADY** was a small
furry monster with two trunks that only
came out at night. She discovered that a
SMOVGROT was a kind of woodlouse jam
and that a **WEENIPWOTCH** was the hairy
tuft between a Huffaluk's toes.

'I win!' gurgled Slop. '957 points
to 106.'

'That's because you got all the
best letters,' huffed Nelly.

'I always win!' gurgled Slop.
'What shall we play now?'

Nelly puffed out her cheeks. She was all gamed out.

She looked around the room for inspiration. Nothing sprang from the white rubber wallpaper and she drew a blank from the white plastic floor too. The clock on the wall said 7.15. Dollop and Splat wouldn't be back for almost two hours.

'Let's play I Spy!' gurgled Slop. 'I Spy with my six yellow eyes …'

'Let's not,' said Nelly.

Slop placed the boot-sale toys back into their bags and returned them to the cupboard under the stairs.

'I know what we can do!' said Nelly, springing off the sofa and turning in the direction of the kitchen.

'What?' gurgled Slop.

'PANCAKES!' said Nelly. 'Do you

like pancakes?'

'How do you play pancakes?' gurgled Slop.

'You don't play 'em, you eat 'em!' said Nelly.
'Have you got any eggs?'

'There'sh loads in the fridge,' gurgled Slop.

'Have you got any milk?'

'Next to the eggs,' gurgled Slop.

'Then pancakes it is!' proclaimed Nelly.

CHAPTER

Nelly marched into the Squurms' kitchen,
feeling quite pleased with herself. Despite Asti's
best efforts to stop her enjoying pancakes at
home she could now enjoy some with Slop.
Even better, with no Asti around she could
nosh as many pancakes as she liked.

Her mum had taught her how to make
them. They were really simple to do.

'I'll need some self-raising flour too, Slop,'
said Nelly, scanning the shiny chrome doors of
the Squurms' kitchen cabinets.

'I don't know what that is, but try in there,'
Slop said, sprouting a feeler from his chest and
spiralling it through the air in the direction of a
cupboard door.

Nelly ran the flats of her fingertips over the
smooth surface of the cupboard. Like the door
under the stairs, there were no handles.

Slop did the honours, opening the cabinet
door with one sucker and the fridge door with
another.

'That looks like flour,' said Nelly, taking a silver packet of soft white powder off the shelf and giving it a sniff. She stuck her finger in and gave it a lick. It tasted sweeter than flour, but Nelly decided to give it a go.

'Eggs,' gurgled Slop.

Nelly turned round and shuddered. Slop was juggling again.

'Careful, Slop, you might drop them!' she gasped.

Slop withdrew all fifteen feelers and let the eggs fall to the floor. They bounced off the floor tiles like super balls and returned to their box.

'What sort of eggs are they?' gasped Nelly.

'They're Veri eggs, of course,' gurgled Slop. 'Haven't you seen a Veri egg before?'

Nelly began to feel foolish for never having seen a Veri egg, and then reminded herself that of course she hadn't seen a Veri egg! She'd never made a pancake for a Squurm before either!

'Let me see one,' said Nelly inquisitively.

Slop tossed an egg to Nelly, who caught it in both hands and cupped it in her palms. It felt about as heavy as an ordinary chicken egg and, if anything, looked slightly whiter.

'What is a Veri?' asked Nelly suspiciously.

'It's a bird, of course!' gurgled Slop. 'It's got three beaks, two at the front of its head, one at the back, and four wings covered in leathers.'

'Don't you mean *feathers*?'

'No, Grimps have *feathers*, Veris have *leathers*. They're kind of leathery feathers. Mum says they're ever so difficult to pluck.'

Nelly nodded blankly and then took a closer look at the egg in her palms. 'How do you crack them open?'

'You don't crack them, you unscrew them,' gurgled Slop, placing two feelers top and bottom of an egg and twisting it in opposite directions.

Nelly watched enthralled as the Veri egg shell parted cleanly to reveal a glistening green yolk inside, about the size of a ping-pong ball. Slop held it under her nose. It smelt just like marzipan.

These were going to be pancakes with a difference!

'All we need now is milk, a mixing bowl and a frying pan!' said Nelly. Slop duly obliged, producing all three at once from three different directions.

Nelly looked at the milk. It was blue. It smelt fresh enough, but it was the colour of a school exercise book. She wasn't at all sure she wanted to know from which creature it had been milked and so instead of asking any further questions she simply poured.

Into the mixing bowl it went, along with the yolks of four Veri eggs and the flour from the silver packet. The mixture went stiff almost instantly.

'More milk!' cried Nelly.

'Coming up,' gurgled Slop.

'More milk again!' cried Nelly. Her arms were already beginning to ache.

'Coming up again!' gurgled Slop. 'Do you want me to whisk?'

Nelly puffed out her cheeks and looked at Slop. The advantage of having twenty arms to whisk with was easy to figure. She handed Slop the bowl with a grateful sigh and carried the frying pan to the cooker. It was an electric one with circular cooking rings, not very different from the one her mum used at home.

'Butter,' said Nelly under her breath. 'I need to melt a knob of ...'

A packet of butter was hovering before her eyes. She reached up and took it from the feeler that was dangling above her head.

'Thank you, Slop,' she said, prising open the packet.

'My pleasure,' gurgled Slop.

The butter was yellow. With black zebra stripes. Nelly smiled adventurously and broke two large chunks into the pan. It sizzled like butter and browned like butter, but the stripes crisped like bacon before dissolving into ash.

'Are you ready with the mixture, Slop?'

Slop gave the mixture a quick whisk with his feelers and then passed the bowl to Nelly.

'Here goes,' said Nelly, pouring in the first measure of pancake mixture.

Slop stood back warily as the frying pan began to sizzle.

'Looking good!' said Nelly, paddling the mixture gently. 'Smells delicious too!'

Slop's nostrils began to twitch as the kitchen filled with the aroma of almonds, peanut butter and strawberry sauce. Nelly lifted the gleaming silver frying pan off the cooker ring and prepared to toss her first ever Squurm pancake.

'Now you have to be careful when you do this, Slop, or your pancake will end up stuck to the ceiling!'

Slop looked up at the ceiling and then back at the frying pan.

'Here goes,' said Nelly, taking the frying pan handle in both hands and getting ready to flip. With a sharp upward jolt Nelly sent the pancake nowhere. It refused to budge. It wasn't stuck to the pan – in fact, it was quite the lightest, fluffiest pancake that Nelly had ever seen. But flip it wouldn't.

Nelly tried again, lowering the frying pan and then hurling it upwards with all her might. But it was no use. She had made the world's first gravity-defying pancake.

'Oh well,' smiled Nelly, placing the frying pan on the side. 'We'll just have to eat it like it is.'

Slop brought two plates down from a cupboard and took some knives and forks out of a drawer. Nelly slid the pancake on to a plate and cut it in half. The smell of strawberry sauce wafted stronger as the pancake divided.

'Half for you, Slop, and half for me!' smiled Nelly.

Slop's orange lava-like body rippled from top to bottom as the first forkful of pancake disappeared inside his lips. Nelly nodded her agreement. The first pancake was delicious. So was the second pancake. In fact, so were the third and the fourth. There was no need for golden syrup or sugar or jam. They were quite sweet enough as they were.

'I think I've had enough pancakes now,' said Nelly with a belch.

'Me too,' gurgled Slop with a squelch. 'What shall we play now?'

'Oh, Slop!' groaned Nelly. 'Aren't you worn out yet?'

'How about hide and seek?' gurgled Slop.

Nelly looked at her watch. There was plenty of time for another game.

'All right, Slop,' she sighed. 'You win. Hide and seek it is.'

CHAPTER 10

'You hide first!' gurgled Slop, his glistening orange body rippling with excitement. 'What shall I count to? A million? A zillion? A frillion?'

'100 will do!' laughed Nelly.

'Forwards or backwards?' gurgled Slop.

'Any way you like!' shouted Nelly, squeezing under the Shredda tank and pressing herself as far back against the wall as she could go. 'And make sure you close your eyes. All six of them!' she shouted.

Slop paused at 43 and a half, placed a sucker over each egg-yolky eye and then proceeded to count upwards to 100 in fractions.

'Coming! Ready or not!!' he gurgled.

'Seen you!' he gurgled again, sending a long
sinuous feeler into the lounge through the
beaded curtain, under the Shredda tank and
tapping Nelly on the nose.

Nelly sighed and wriggled out from her hiding place.

'How can you possibly see me when you're not even in the same room?' she protested.

'Your pulse gave you away!' gurgled Slop. 'I win!'

Nelly stood up and put her hands on her hips.

'You don't win. It just means it's your turn to hide and my turn to seek.'

'Close your eyes and count to a hundred then!' gurgled Slop. 'I'm gloing to hide.'

Nelly cupped her hands over her eyes and began to count. She kept her ears open for clues but heard nothing except the sound of her own voice.

'Ninety-eight, ninety-nine, one hundred! Coming! Ready or not!' she called.

The house fell silent.

Nelly turned in the direction of the curtain and slid her hands through the beads. They parted with a soft jangle as she made her way through into the lounge.

Her eyes dropped to the floor beneath the green plastic curtains hanging either side of the bay window. Slop wasn't hiding there.

'Too obvious,' she murmured, skirting around the armchairs and then dropping to her knees to see if Slop had squeezed under the tiny gap beneath the sofa. He wasn't hiding there either.

She padded barefoot across the rubber
carpet tiles and prised open the door of the
games cupboard. There was no sign of the little
orange rascal in there either.

She frowned and took ten determined strides into the kitchen. She squinted into the narrow gaps between the units. She even prised open the kitchen cupboards with a fork. The shelves were lined with groceries of the grossest kind: tins of Squeek liver in bitter bean sauce, pickled Jov cheeks, Mungus steaks, boil in the bag Lumpit and family packets of Odd in batter were piled high. But there was no sign of Slop.

Nelly scratched her head. She was beginning to sense that she had a challenge on her hands. Wherever Slop was hiding, you could be sure that he wasn't going to be easy to find. She opened the fridge door and lifted the flap of the freezer compartment. The space inside was already occupied. Not by Slop, but by a packet of frozen Weeps.

She closed the fridge and turned towards the bin, placed her foot on the red chromium pedal and pressed down. The lid flapped open to reveal the leftovers from the Squurms' tea the night before: four fish eyes the size of cricket balls and a scattering of cactus peelings.

Slop wasn't in the lounge and he wasn't in the kitchen. So where was he?

'I'm going to find you, Slop! If it's the last

thing I do!' she shouted.

She paused for a moment, half-hoping that Slop might acknowledge her with a gurgle and give her a clue as to where he was hiding.

No such luck.

Maybe he's sneaked upstairs, she thought. *I know, I'll check the cupboard under the stairs, and if he's not in there I'll look in the bedrooms.*

Nelly left the kitchen and returned to the hallway. She passed the flats of her hands across the door of the cupboard under the stairs and then knocked on it loudly, twice.

'Slop, if you're hiding in there it's not fair because I can't open the door without suckers, so come out right now if you ARE in there!'

Nelly waited. And listened. And sighed.

'I'll try upstairs.'

There were fifteen steps to climb. All of them felt strangely spongy underfoot. *They must use marshmallow instead of underlay,* thought Nelly. She stopped for a moment and flicked her eyes between three doors. Two were the colour of mushy peas, the third was the colour of oxtail soup.

As she stepped towards the third door, it slid automatically to her left. She stepped into the room and looked down at a gently sloping mustard-coloured mosaic floor. In the middle of the floor was a huge brass plug hole about the size of a dustbin lid. Around the green rubber walls, rows upon rows of jacuzzi jets were pointing at her from all levels and directions.

It was a shower room with enough jet power to clean a fleet of tractors.

Pink fluffy towels hung from a blue towel rail to her left and a huge piece of soggy black soap lay glistening in one corner of the floor. There was no bath and there was no Slop.

Nelly scratched her chin and headed for the bedrooms. 'I'm getting warmer, Slop!' she called half-hopefully.

The first of the mushy pea coloured bedroom doors slid back and Nelly peered tentatively into the room.

Tins of coloured eye shadow were scattered across the floor and a paintbrush was propped up in front of a wall-length mirror to her left. It was Splat and Dollop's bedroom.

A photograph of Slop as a chrysalis hung in a gilt frame by the window and a large double bed lay propped up against the opposite wall.

Not flat to the floor like a normal bed but fixed vertically to the wall.

'Squurms must sleep standing up!' Nelly gasped.

Her inquisitive nature suddenly gave way
to a slight pang of guilt. She wasn't at all sure
that she should be snooping around Splat
and Dollop's bedroom. After all, bedrooms
were private in her own house and she saw no
reason why they should be any different in a
Squurm's home. Anyway, something told her
Slop wouldn't be hiding in here. She scanned
the room quickly and moved on.

As she approached the second green door it
slid open to reveal Slop's bedroom.

'Are you in here, Slop?' she called, placing
her hands on the door frame and peeking
inside. Sure enough, a smaller bed was fixed
securely and vertically to the far wall. The
décor was the same. White rubber floor tiles,
yellow perspex walls. There were few places to

hide except for a small aluminium cupboard positioned directly below the bedroom window.

Nelly crept into the room, crouched down and ran her fingers across the cupboard doors.

'Are you in there, Slop?' she whispered.

To her relief, the doors slid open. But to her dismay, music began playing. It was a hi-fi unit. A Slop-less hi-fi unit at that.

Nelly began to feel uneasy. She sighed heavily and looked at her watch. It was 8.35. Splat and Dollop would be home soon and she still had the washing up to do!

Enough was enough. She had hunted high and low and Slop was nowhere to be found. Reluctantly, she would have to concede defeat again.

'He's probably squeezed up a tap or something,' sighed Nelly. 'Anything to win.'

'All right, Slop!' she cried. 'You win again! Your mum and dad will be home soon. It's time to stop playing and start tidying! You can come out now!'

Nelly waited for a loud gurgle and the reappearance of a victorious Slop. But neither happened. She walked to the top of the stairs and cleared her throat.

'I SAID IT'S TIME TO STOP PLAYING NOW, SLOP! YOU CAN COME OUT NOW, WHEREVER YOU ARE!!'

But Slop didn't come out. The house remained as eerily silent as ever.

Nelly frowned and walked down the stairs. Why wasn't Slop answering? Why hadn't he stopped hiding? Where could he be?

'The sandpit!' she gasped. 'What if he's been sucked into the sandpit?'

Nelly raced down the hallway, scooted through the lounge and charged out into the garden.

She pelted to the lip of the sandpit and stared at the surface of the quicksand for signs of entry.

All was still.

'ARE YOU IN THERE, SLOP? IF YOU'RE IN THERE, COME OUT RIGHT NOW!!'

She stared down at her toes. 'I can't go in again, it's far too dangerous! Surely Slop wouldn't have hidden in here?'

A thought too terrifying to contemplate iced her veins.

The Shreddas! Maybe he's fallen into the Shredda tank!

She spun round hard and sprinted back into the house.

With a desperate lunge, she pressed her face hard to the glass of the aquarium. The pack of Shreddas flew out from behind the bricks and barked ferociously, just centimetres from her face. Nelly ignored them completely and scanned every millilitre of the aquarium for signs of chewed-up Slop.

To her relief there were none to be seen.

she hollered.

But still there was no reply.

This wasn't a game any more. It had stopped being a game some time ago. This was no fun at all, full stop. Nelly had promised the Squurms that Slop would be in safe hands, but she had absolutely no idea where he was! She double-checked the kitchen, the lounge, the hallway and upstairs. She even went up into the loft. She called Slop's name from the front door in both directions. She knocked hard again on the cupboard under the stairs, she even looked up her own sleeves. But there was no sign of him anywhere.

'What am I going to do?' she groaned. 'Splat and Dollop will be home in ten minutes and I haven't just lost my trainers and socks, I've lost their son!'

'SLOPPPPP!!! WHERE ARE YOUUUUUUUU!!!!!!!' she cried.

But there was no reply.

Nelly squished down on to the sofa and racked her brains. She had looked absolutely everywhere she could think of. There was no time to ring any of her monster friends for help either. It was eight minutes and counting before Dollop and Splat would return. She was on her own, in every sense.

She stood up dejectedly and tidied up a few games that were still scattered across the lounge floor. With a puff of her cheeks she trudged barefoot into the kitchen and began stacking the washing-up beside the sink.

'What am I going to say to Dollop and Splat?' she whimpered, placing the plug into its hole and turning the taps. 'They're going to go bananas.'

One by one she placed the plates, mixing bowl and frying pan into the water.

She took off her watch, glanced at the minute hand and reached for the Furry Liquid. With a dejected squirt and a swish of her hand she began cleaning the dishes with a scourer. She was in a daze. How could she possibly have lost Slop? The front door of the house had been closed and she'd only shut her eyes for a count of 100.

With a dispirited sigh, Nelly reached for the tea towel and began drying. She stacked the plates neatly to one side and then glanced again at her watch. Only three minutes and counting.

She dried the mixing bowl and then inspected it for traces of pancake mix. Satisfied that it was clean, she returned it to the cupboard. Two minutes and counting.

With a blink and a sniff, Nelly picked up the frying pan and began wiping it dry with the cloth. She buffed the chromium base of the pan to a brilliant sparkle and then held it out for a final inspection. She tilted it first one way and then the other.

She frowned. There was a reflection in the pan that she couldn't quite account for. It was orange, it had yellow blobs in it and the black smiling shape of a mouth.

Nelly's eyes sprang upwards. There, directly above her head, was Slop, clinging like a pancake to the ceiling!

'I WIN, Nelly!' he gurgled.

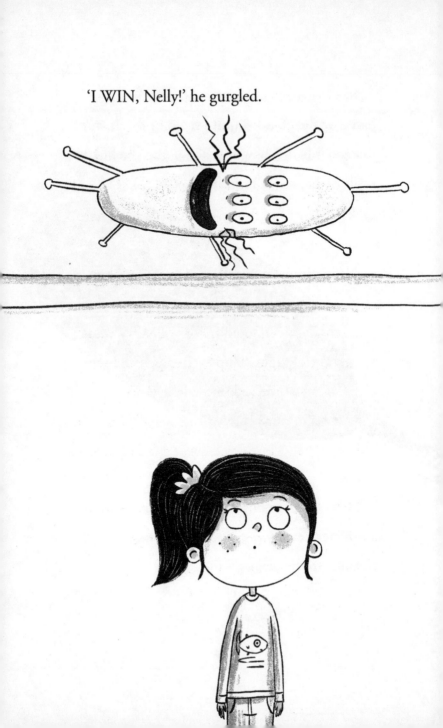

'It was you that gave me the idea to hide up here. You never found me, did you, Nelly? I've been watching you walk backwards and forwards, looking and looking and looking and looking. It was so funny because I was up here all the time!'

Nelly didn't know whether to squonk him or hit him with the frying pan.

'Slop, I've been looking for you everywhere!'

'I know!' gurgled Slop excitedly. 'I've been watching you! You've hunted low, you've hunted high, but you didn't hunt high enough, did you, Nelly? I told you I was good at hide and seek! I told you I would win!'

The sound of a toilet flushing suddenly drew Nelly's attention to the front door. Dollop and Splat had returned!

They slithered in, carrying a king-size bucket of toffee popcorn.

'We bought this for you, Nelly. We hope you like it!' Splat gurgled.

'*Jafukoog!*' said Nelly. '*Jafukoog* very much!'

Splat looked at Dollop in complete puzzlement. 'I'm sorry, Nelly, what did you say?'

'I said *jafukoog*,' said Nelly. '*Jafukoog* is Squurmese for "*thank you*", isn't it?'

'There's no such word, Nelly!' chuckled Dollop. 'You haven't been playing Scrabble with Slop, have you?'

'Among other things,' said Nelly, turning to Slop with a glare.

Slop gurgled sweetly and smiled at his mum and dad. 'We've had a fantastic time! We've played loads of games! Nelly's ever so glood at coming second!'

'We've had a wonderful time too, thanks to you, Nelly,' gurgled Dollop. 'We had the whole cinema to ourselves! Everyone got up and left just as we walked in!'

Nelly smiled wearily. She was exhausted. One thing she wouldn't be doing when she got home was playing games. She wasn't even sure she'd have the energy to fill in her secret monster-sitting notebook.

'I'll be off then!' smiled Nelly, offering Dollop and Splat a goodbye handshake.

Her offer was declined in favour of a cold wet squonk on the cheek from Dollop and a double squonk on the nose from Slop.

'Come and play again, won't you, Nelly!'

'ZIBBLFLUDGE,' said Nelly, with a nod and a wink.

Slop scratched his head with four feelers and looked up at his parents. Nelly closed the gate behind her and then smiled as the long extended feeler that she had been expecting spiralled down the path and tapped her on the shoulder. It belonged, of course, to Slop.

'What does ZIBBLFLUDGE mean?' he shouted.

'It's Nelly-ese for "NEXT TIME I WIN!"' laughed Nelly.

LOOK OUT FOR THE NEXT

ADVENTURE

COMING SOON